THE
GOOD SAMARITAN
AND OTHER FAVORITE BIBLE STORIES

Illustrations by Don Page
Retold by Laura Kelly

The Good Samaritan   Luke 10:25-37

A man who knew God's law said to Jesus, "I know that I should love God with all my heart. I know that I should love my neighbor as myself. But I have a question for you. Just who is my neighbor?"

Jesus answered the man's question by telling him a story:
   An Israelite was once walking on the road from Jerusalem
to Jericho. Robbers beat him up and took all that he had.

A priest came down the road. When he saw the hurt man, he crossed to the other side of the road and walked on by. Another man came down the road. He also crossed to the other side and passed by the hurt man without stopping to help.

Then a Samaritan came down the road. Samaritans and Israelites were not friendly to one another. But when the Samaritan saw the hurt man, he wanted to help him. The Samaritan put the Israelite on his donkey and took him to an inn. He stayed there with the Israelite and took care of him.

"Now," said Jesus, "which of the travelers was a neighbor to the hurt man?"

"The one who was kind to him," said the man who knew God's law.

The Lost Sheep Luke 15:1-7

Jesus also told this story:

A shepherd had one hundred sheep. He loved his sheep and took very good care of them. Every night, as the sheep went into their pen, the shepherd counted to make sure they were there. One night, the shepherd counted only ninety-nine. One sheep was missing!

The shepherd went to look for the missing sheep. He searched the whole countryside. And when the shepherd found his sheep, he was joyful! He told all his neighbors the good news.

Jesus said that God is like that shepherd. He loves his people very much.

The Prodigal Son Luke 15:11-31

Here is another story Jesus told:

There was a man who had two sons. The younger one was tired of living at home. He wanted to see the world. "I want to go away," he said to his father. "Please give me my share of the family fortune now."

The father was sad, but he gave his son the money. The young man went far away. He bought expensive things and did anything he wanted. Soon he had no money left, not even money for food.

The young man found a job feeding pigs. He was so hungry that even the pigs' food began to look good to him. He thought about his home. "Why did I leave?" he asked himself. "Back at my father's house, even the hired men have more than enough to eat. I was not a good son, but maybe my father will take me back as a servant."

The young man headed home. When he was still a long way off, his father saw him coming. The father ran to meet his son and give him a big hug. Then the father said to the servants, "Let's have a party. My son has come home!"

Jesus said that God loves his children as the father loved his son.